Franklin
Plays the Game

Scholastic Children's Books
Commonwealth House, 1-19 New Oxford Street
London WC1A 1NU
a division of Scholastic Ltd

London ~ New York ~ Toronto ~ Sydney
Mexico City ~ New Delhi ~ Hong Kong

First published in Canada by Kids Can Press, Toronto, 1995
First published in the UK by Scholastic Ltd, 2000

Franklin is a trademark of Kids Can Press Ltd.
Text copyright © 1995 by P.B. Creations Inc.
Illustrations copyright © 1995 by Brenda Clark Illustrator Inc.

Published by permission of Kids Can Press Ltd., Toronto, Ontario, Canada.

ISBN: 0 439 01439 5

Printed in Hong Kong

10 9 8 7 6 5 4 3 2 1

Franklin
Plays the Game

Written by Paulette Bourgeois
Illustrated by Brenda Clark

Hippo

Franklin could slide down a river bank. He could tie his shoes and count by twos. He could walk to Bear's house all by himself. But Franklin couldn't kick a football straight. That was a problem because Franklin wanted to be the best player on his team.

Franklin loved football. He liked the running
and the dribbling. He especially liked the strips. He
wore his purple and yellow shirt and matching shin
pads, even when he wasn't playing football.

Sometimes he slept with his ball and dreamed
of scoring goals.

Before every game, Franklin practised in the park.
He kicked the ball with the inside of his foot again
and again. He did warm-up stretches and cool-down walks.

Still, Franklin had trouble. He couldn't run very fast,
even without a football at his feet. And when Franklin
kicked the ball, it never went where he intended it to.

Goose watched Franklin's ball fly into the bushes.
"I'll never score a goal," said Franklin sadly.
"Neither will I," said Goose. "I keep forgetting the
rule that says I cannot use my wings unless I'm the
goalkeeper. Everyone gets cross with me."
Goose showed Franklin how wide her wings
stretched out.

Beaver was watching, too.

"And I'll never score a goal," she said, "because my tail is so long and heavy that it drags me down."

She ran for a bit. Franklin and Goose could see the problem.

"No wonder we never win any of our games," grumbled Franklin.

It was true. Franklin's team had not won a game all season. Bear's team won every game.

Losing didn't bother Coach. She said the same thing before each game, "Let's have fun out there!"

Losing didn't bother Franklin's parents, who shouted, "Nice try!" whenever Franklin got the ball.

But losing bothered Franklin a lot.

"What's wrong?" asked Franklin's father.

"I never score any goals," answered Franklin.

"But you try and you have fun," said Franklin's father. "That's the important thing."

Franklin nodded. That's what all the grown-ups said. But he really wanted everybody to be cheering for him. He wanted to score a goal!

It wasn't only Franklin who felt that way. All of Franklin's friends wanted to score a goal too. But the harder they tried, the worse they played. Franklin forgot where to stand. Goose forgot what to do.

Whenever the ball came to Franklin's team-mates, they rushed towards it. They tripped over their feet and tails and long ears and landed in a heap!

Coach helped to untangle them. "You have to work together as a team. You have to share the ball."

But it wasn't easy to do. Their team lost again.
It made the players feel sad. Franklin huddled inside
his shell. Beaver tucked in her tail and Goose folded
her wings.

The other team crossed the field to shake hands.

"Nice try," said Bear.
Franklin didn't come out of his shell.
Bear bounced the football up and down.
"Come on out, Franklin," said Bear.

Franklin poked his head out just as Bear's ball
was coming up. Franklin bounced the ball off
the top of his head. It went flying straight to Goose.
She spread her wings.
"Saved!" Franklin shouted.

Beaver was so excited that she flapped her tail up and down.

"That's it!" cried Franklin.

"What's it?" asked Bear.

Franklin smiled at Beaver and Goose. "I think I know how we can score goals," he said, patting his head. "But it will take some teamwork."

Every day until the next game, Franklin and the team practised in the park. Coach helped them to work on some special moves.

They giggled and laughed and dribbled and bounced.

They played in the rain and slid in the mud.

One day, Bear came past. "What are you doing?" he asked.

"Just having fun," said Franklin. He could hardly wait until the next game.

It was time for the final game. The team-mates
huddled together.

"Let's show them what we can do," said Franklin.

But within the first minutes of the game, Bear's
team scored a goal.

"Team," said Coach, "it's time for your special moves."
Goose went into goal. She used her wings as much
as she wanted to and made three spectacular saves.
The crowd cheered.

Goose spotted Franklin on the field and tossed the ball to him. It landed on Franklin's head. With a strong header, Franklin sent the ball soaring over to Beaver. With a swish of her tail, Beaver passed the ball to Rabbit. He lifted his big foot and kicked the ball into the net. Franklin's team had scored!

The team-mates jumped for joy and hugged one another.

For the rest of the game, they played their best. Franklin even headed the ball twice, but nobody on his team scored again. Bear's team scored once more and won the game.

Coach gave all of her players a rosette.

"You should be proud of yourselves," she said. "You worked hard as a team. You ALL helped to score that goal."

Franklin's parents invited the team out for a treat.
"Why?" asked Franklin. "Our team didn't win."
"You look like winners to us," said his father.
Franklin agreed. They were tired and dirty and
happy. All the signs of a winning team!